BERKSHIRE
SEASONS OF CELEBRATION

PHOTOGRAPHS BY

Niki Berg • Joel Librizzi
Jane McWhorter • Beverly Pabst

TEXT BY

Katharine H. Annin • Gerard Chapman
Richard Nunley

FOREWORD BY

Lawrence K. Miller

EDITED BY

Sam Bittman and Steven A. Satullo

Either/Or Press

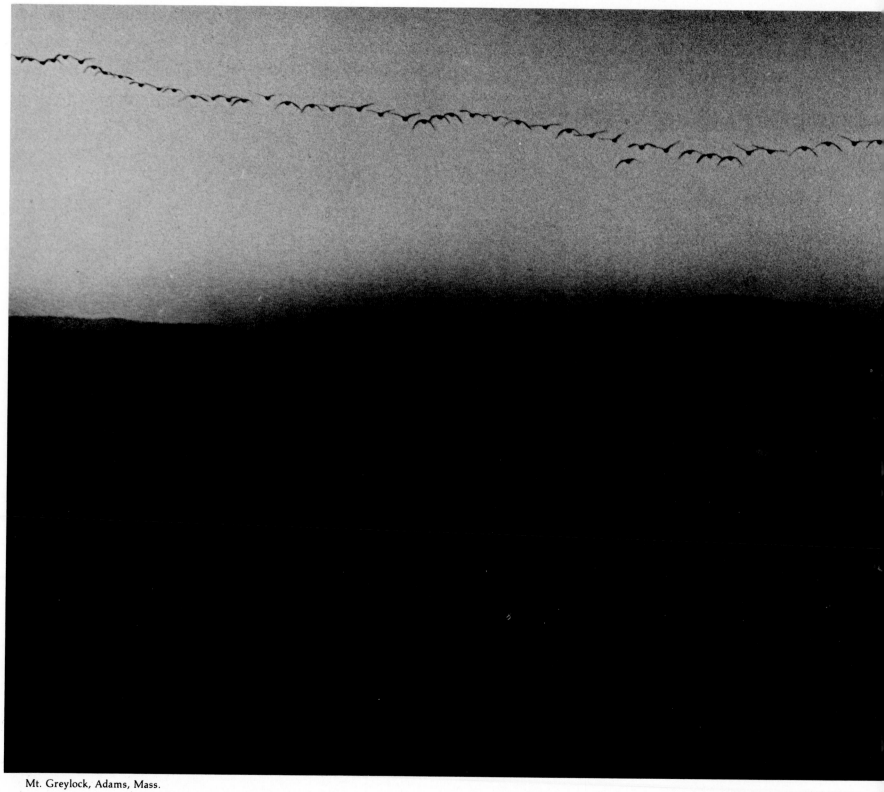

Mt. Greylock, Adams, Mass.

FOREWORD

I rejoice that adaptations of some of Katharine Annin's and Richard Nunley's columns in *The Berkshire Eagle* are now in book form. For 25 years Kay Annin's gentle observations on Berkshire life have graced our Op-Ed page. Dick Nunley's memoirs have appeared for a much shorter period. This gives promise that these essays on Berkshire themes will continue regularly on newsprint into the next century, but more important that many of their most evocative past efforts will be preserved in less perishable and more readily available form.

Similarly, the columns of Gerard Chapman whose researches into local history have given solid factual and biographical grounding of past significant Berkshire events and notable lives are a source of editorial satisfaction. He has been painstaking in checking sources, sometimes revealing discrepancies in the records available, and always objective in his presentation. Chapman has set the stage for the more subjective reflections of his co-contributors who discourse about this glorious realm, its wonders large and small, and its not overpowering ironies.

It has been editorial policy of *The Eagle* for more than 40 years to search out and encourage Berkshire full- or part-time residents of facile pen to contribute on some regular basis to the newspaper on regional concerns not necessarily reported in the news columns. They have written about natural history, the changing seasons, rural problems, village issues and the chemistry of change hastened by human intervention, sometimes benign, sometimes harsh. Many others have preceded the three contemporary writers presented here in a department called "Our Berkshires" whose logo first appeared in 1940. They have been naturalists, horticulturalists, farmers, teachers, conservationists, clergymen, historians and sportsmen. I hesitate to name them all lest I fail to recall those of brilliant plumage who were birds of passage.

Whatever prompted this policy originally in a small-city newspaper is of small moment other than celebrating the area's scenic charm and natural resources. But the opening of our columns to such writers has made increasing editorial sense as newspapers have had to share their hard news monopoly with the electronic media. As commercial television and radio necessarily have sought in their non-news time slots primarily to entertain, it has made it possible for newspapers, which so choose, to please a readership surfeited by this junk-food diet.

The audience for such writing has always been there, though small by mass electronic communication standards. It has been literate and loyal, thoughtful and appreciative. It is my hope they will respond to the appeal of this volume by a reinforced affection through reading their raptures made visually more legible and thus the more compelling.

Lawrence K. Miller, publisher
The Berkshire Eagle

New Year's Day

Hancock, Mass.

I'd love to be a winter-coated cow
Chewing my cud slowly in the bright sun
Out of the wind by the side of the barn,
Head hung down at just the comfort level,
Breath rising in short-lived visible puffs,
Hearing my mates shift and blow around me,
My bulgy flank hot under ice-cold hair.

I'd love the stiffened softness underfoot
Where the cold congeals the hoof-dented mud
Edged with still-green grass where the snow begins
And takes off waltzing down the pasture slope
To willows turning orange by the creek
Like minor nimbuses against the slate
Of woods and hills a field or two away.

I'd love to stare long at the round snow cap
Delicately heaped to the maximum
On the electric fence insulator
Nailed to the deep-grained post (more by the wire
Held up than holding it), its pauseful clicks
Pulsing the sun and afternoon away
With the wistful transience of always.

Bounding down the salted road, skiers' cars
Would drizzle toward the city, and inside
Farmer with his feet up after dinner
Would watch football on TV, but, a cow,
I'd love my placid productivity
And slowly chew and stare while purple light
And chillness overtook the timeless air.

— Richard Nunley

CELEBRATE
WINTER TO WINTER

PHOTOGRAPHS BY
JOEL LIBRIZZI

TEXT BY
GERARD CHAPMAN

Pittsfield, Mass.

OUR BERKSHIRE PAST

The great Pittsfield-Lenox shire-town war

When in 1812 Pittsfield made its first attempt to secure the county government, a group of its citizens memorialized the legislature, averring that it was "an incontrovertible fact that this town is more conveniently situated for the transaction of all concerns in the courts of law and in the public offices than the town of Lenox." They offered "to erect pleasant and suitable buildings at their own expense" and appointed a committee to examine the subject for a report to the legislature. Their report called for a lot of not less than one acre, a well-built courthouse with two jury rooms and fireproof offices, and a jail, and for compensation to Lenox of $2,666. They even raised $9,000 of the $14,000 estimated costs to effect the transfer. When the question was considered by the spring session of the legislature in 1814, the towns of Lanesboro, Dalton, Hinsdale, Washington, Peru, Savoy and Adams lent their support by petitions.

But in Lenox 20 citizens girded their loins in opposition, asserting that "while they lived, Lenox should remain the county seat." The whole town supported them, and when the matter was decided, the vote of Richmond swung the issue in favor of Lenox. So it was that in 1816 the new courthouse in Lenox was erected, a handsome building designed by Isaac Damon of Northampton. It is now the Lenox Library.

And so the situation remained until a new effort was made in 1826 to remove the center of county government to Pittsfield, but it was short-lived and ineffective.

The Western Railroad having been completed in 1842, Pittsfield assumed greater importance, and in April of 1843 the matter of removal was placed before the people of the county in a referendum, but the deplorable condition of the roads militated against the effort, and again Lenox succeeded in retaining the county government.

By 1854 the Housatonic Railroad had reached Pittsfield from the south, affording easy access to it from the towns of South Berkshire and the question was agitated once again. This time around even Great Barrington, on the far side of Lenox, gave Pittsfield its support. The topic was discussed heatedly throughout the county and debated in the press; committees were formed, petitions circulated and resolutions presented to the legislature; and finally that body put before the several town meetings the question: "Do you desire a removal of the courts from Lenox; and if so, name the town or towns to which they shall be removed." Pittsfield, of course, voted all but unanimously for itself, and some towns for double county seats at Pittsfield and Great Barrington, but the great majority favored retaining the courthouse and associated facilities in Lenox. Once again Lenox had triumphed, but its days were numbered.

For in 1868 it had become evident to all that Pittsfield was indisputably the center of county life. When the proposition was once more revived, there was little but token opposition. The legislature voted to make the long-sought change on the condition that adequate facilities be provided for the several government departments until a suitable courthouse and jail could be built.

They paid John Chandler Williams $35,000 for his land on the corner of Park Square and East Street, and of the $350,000 that the legislature appropriated, $190,000 was for the jail and $160,000 for the courthouse. Louis Weisbein of Boston designed the buildings, and the courthouse, constructed of marble from Chester Goodale's quarry in Sheffield, was completed in 1871. The jail on Second Street was built of pressed brick with some marble.

Berkshire roots of the women's movement

Although Susan B. Anthony and her sister crusaders fought for women's right to vote in the last half of the 19th century, the social and sexual revolution of recent years, as well as the continuing effort to achieve passage of the Equal Rights Amendment, foster the impression that women's struggle to realize an equal status with men is merely a contemporary phenomenon.

But over the centuries, the more outspoken or daring women have expressed discontent with their subsidiary role and, indeed, their almost total lack of legal rights. It is interesting to look back through the pages of that venerable weekly newspaper in Great Barrington, *The Berkshire Courier*, and find that women there deplored their subservience in both prose and poetry.

For example, in the issue of Oct. 31, 1867, there is a long essay by one Gail Hamilton covering the many aspects of life in her day that she felt placed her and her sisters in situations servile to men.

She railed against unequal pay for equivalent work:

"A female assistant in a high school, a woman of education, refinement, accomplishments, tact and sense, receives $600, and if she stays 600 years, she will receive no more. A male assistant, fresh from a college or normal school, thoroughly unseasoned, without elegance of manners, or dignity of presence or experience . . . receives $1,000. His thousand is because he is a man. Her six hundred is because she is a woman. Her little finger may be worth more to the school than his whole body, but that goes for nothing."

Ms. Hamilton wrote that more than 100 years ago, but today's women voice the same complaint. They say, *plus ça change, plus c'est la même chose.*

In the issue of Nov. 16, 1881, an anonymous woman condemns the double standard by which the transgressions of men and women were regarded. From her free-verse poem titled "Stone The Woman," we excerpt a few lines by which she makes her point:

Yes, stone the woman — let the man go free;
Let one soul suffer the guilt of two —
Is the doctrine of the hurried world,
Too out of breath for holding balances
Where nice distinctions and injustices
Are calmly weighed. But, ah, how will it be
On that strange day of fire and flame,
When men shall stand before the one
True Judge? Shall sex make then
A difference in sin? Shall He . . .
Condemn the woman and forgive the man?

In this area, there has been some degree, at least, of mitigation of that harsh distinction without a difference.

James A. Garfield: Berkshire's president-poet

In the summer of 1854, before Williams College opened, James A. Garfield looked up some of his cousins in Monterey, in South Berkshire. Says one of his biographers, Theodore Clarke Smith, late professor of history at Williams:

"It was his first introduction to a New England farming community and to the cheerful, companionable but unambitious stock from which his father had sprung . . . There [were] some 20 or 30 families of them . . . settled Yankee farmers, tilling their stony fields and living content in their village surroundings. He was ambitious for intellectual triumphs and steeped in sentiment. It is doubtful if Thomas, Solomon, Daniel or Elijah Garfield of Monterey, ever thought of the Berkshire Hills as 'cloud-capped mountains propping the bending heavens,' and James Garfield would have nothing less."

Then, as now, *The Courier*, published in Great Barrington, reported news of the surrounding towns, of which Monterey, contiguous on the east, is one. In the issue of Aug. 24, 1854, appeared a poem of 63 rhymed lines in seven stanzas titled "Morning in Berkshire," by Hattie A. Pease. Her first stanza, as a sample:

I love to wander forth at early dawn
'Neath thy green trees, still wet with
*   pearly showers*
And list the breeze with steps so like
*   a fawn*
Steal softly by to kiss the sleeping
*   flowers.*
This world is fairest seen at morning hours;
While yet the day so innocent, and young,
Peeps shyly forth from Night's lone sombre
*   bow'rs,*
Her morning robes of gray around her flung;

And o'er her blushing face, a 'misty night-cap
*   hung.'*

In the next issue of the paper, just a week later, appeared the poem "To 'Hattie'"; it was signed "A Stranger." Garfield, according to a later editor of *The Courier*, was said to have composed it sitting atop Mount Peter, a rocky eminence within the village of Great Barrington. His first few lines:

The western sun had sought his ocean bed
Behind the granite hills, and sable night
Had spread her raven wing wide o'er the world,
When first I gazed upon the evening star
From this, the lovely village, where perchance
Thy home is, Hattie, though I know it not,
*   nor thee.*

As is well-known, Garfield became president and after four months in office was shot by Charles J. Guiteau on July 2, 1881, and died on Sept. 19.

Turning again to *The Courier* (July 13, 1881), we read under the heading "Monterey's Fourth" that two days after Guiteau's shot, the townsfolk had "assembled in the grove" beside Brewer Pond for speeches, games and celebration of the nation's birthday, and that ". . . it having been suggested, the question was introduced, what shall we name this lake? Some favored 'Lake Brewer' while others favored 'Lake Garfield,' and the latter name appearing to have the preference, it was voted that hereafter it is to be known as 'Lake Garfield,' and if the president recovers, a telegram be sent him apprising him of the same."

The name has endured and is so indicated on all modern maps of the area. Further research reveals there are no longer any of the Garfield name resident in the town.

Agrippa Hull . . . "a sort of Sancho Panza . . ."

One of the most colorful characters in the Stockbridge of old was Agrippa Hull, a gentleman of color who by his dignity and wit endeared himself to all, and was affectionately known as "Grippy."

He was born March 7, 1759, in Northampton, whether of slaves or freemen is uncertain, as slavery in Massachusetts was not abolished until the adoption of the state constitution in 1780. But he does seem to have been free upon his arrival in Stockbridge at age six, in company with one Joab, who had been freed to become the servant of Jonathan Edwards, minister there since 1751. Little is known about Agrippa Hull's life until his enlistment in 1777 in the local militia for service in the Revolutionary War.

He became orderly to Col. (later Maj.-Gen.) John Paterson of Lenox and served him for two years. Says that officer's biographer, Thomas Egleston, of Agrippa Hull, ". . . he was intelligent and unusually bright. His aptness and wit and his readiness in repartee, as well as the intelligent manner in which he performed all his duties, made him a great favorite with all the officers . . ."

So much so, in fact, that Thaddeus Kosciusko, the Polish general who joined our Revolution in 1777, ". . . took a fancy to Grippy, and after a time became much attached to him." Col. Paterson gave his services to the Pole, who "made Grippy his confidential and head servant, and put him in charge of his wardrobe. The general had brought with him from Poland a costly uniform, said to have been brilliant with adornments." There is the oft-told tale of Grippy dressing himself in the resplendent outfit during its owner's absence and hosting a party in the general's tent for the orderlies of the other officers, only to have the general return unexpectedly. Gen. Kosciusko took the transgression in good humor, but paraded his crestfallen servant before the encampment. Never again did Grippy take such a liberty, but in his later years he delighted in telling the story to his host of young friends in Stockbridge.

When Gen. Kosciusko returned to Poland after the war, he wanted to take his orderly with him; not wishing to cross his employer, Grippy agreed to go but ran away to avoid actually leaving his country. However, when Gen. Kosciusko returned to America for a visit in 1797, and Agrippa journeyed to New York to meet him, the reunion was affectionate.

After having served in the Continental Army for six years and two months, Agrippa Hull was mustered out at West Point and returned to Stockbridge. There he became a butler in the home of Theodore Sedgwick, and when that most renowned lawyer and judge of Berkshire County went to Washington to serve in both the House and Senate in the first Congress of the new nation, he took Agrippa Hull with him.

During his years in the Army, Agrippa

Hull had also become acquainted with the Marquis de Lafayette, and during a visit of the Frenchman to America after the war, the Sedgwicks took him to New York to meet the general.

After Judge Sedgwick had freed the celebrated "Mum Bet" by citing the freedom clause in the new state constitution, Agrippa prevailed upon his employer to secure the freedom of Jane Darby, a slave of a Mr. Ingersoll of Lenox, who thereupon became his wife. After she died, he married (in 1813), Margaret Timbroke, called Peggy. The pair combined talents; hers was the making of wedding cakes, gingerbread and root beer, and his the efficient management of elaborate social functions. Electa Jones who wrote the earliest history of Stockbridge in 1854, averred that "his presence at weddings seemed almost a necessity."

They lived on several acres of land on the Old County Road (now Route 7), and in Margaret French Cresson's book, *The Laurel Hill Association*, the map identifies the present-day Konkapot Brook as being also called "Peggy's Brook."

Agrippa Hull's fame spread beyond Stockbridge, and when the eminent historian Francis Parkman visited there in 1844, he interviewed the old man. That same year his appearance was preserved for us when Col. Henry Wright took him to West Stockbridge, where Anson Clark made a daguerreotype picture of him. A later (unknown) artist, using that picture as a source, painted him in oils, and both the picture and the painting are in the Historical Room of the Stockbridge Library. In 1973, at an exhibition in Washington titled "The Black Presence in the Era of the American Revolution, 1770-1800," the picture was hung prominently, and it also appears in a booklet describing the event.

Catharine Sedgwick, the doyenne of Stockbridge letters, is quoted in her biographical compendium of *Life and Letters*, (edited by Mary E. Dewey, 1871), as saying, "Grippy is one of the few who will be immortal in our village annals . . . He had a fund of humor and mother wit, and was a sort of Sancho Panza in the village, always trimming other men's follies with a keen perception, and the biting wit of wisdom. Grippy was a capital subaltern, but a very poor officer. As a servant he was faultless, but in his own domain at home a tyrant."

In a pithy bit of self-evaluation, he once remarked, "It is not the cover of the book, but what the book contains is the question. Many a good book has a dark cover."

When Agrippa Hull died on May 21, 1848, Stockbridge lost one of its favorite personalities.

William Pitt Palmer's literary "Smack . . ."

During a good part of the past century, a prominent Berkshire poet was William Pitt Palmer who, like several others, has largely sunk from sight. That he was a Berkshire native was quite by chance; his father, a farmer-soldier of the Revolution whose ancestors came from Nottinghamshire in 1629, and his mother, were on the way from Stonington, Conn., to their new home in Stockbridge when they stopped in that town just over the line from South Lee, and there the boy was born Feb. 22, 1805. Shortly afterward they moved on to the center of town. On old maps, three Palmer farms are shown to have been on what is now Mahkeenac Road just north of the Turnpike overpass, and from their home there the youngster walked about 3/4 mile to a traditional "little red schoolhouse." At the age of 10, he was sent to the Academy on the Plain, of which Jared Curtis was the master.

William Pitt Palmer was best known for the least "literary" of his verse, the comic poem "The Smack in School," the locale of which was the Little Red Schoolhouse. On early maps, it is shown to have been situated on what is now Larrywaug — Prospect Hill Road just west of its junction with the old road to Interlaken, now designated Hill Road (and cut by the Turnpike). At some undetermined time, it was moved around the corner onto what is now North Church Street and was incorporated into the home now owned by Capt. and Mrs. John S. Kilner, where it serves as their living room. The poem seems to have first appeared in a Pittsfield journal with the long name of *The Farmer, the Berkshire Culturist, the Horticulturist and Mechanic*, in its issue of Nov. 15, 1858, and was reprinted in the *Pittsfield Sun* three days later.

The poem achieved great popular success and, appearing in school texts over several years, was a favorite piece for recitation on visitors' days. It told of a bashful country boy, William Willis, who one day in school kissed Susannah Pease with a resounding smack. Hailed up front to the schoolmaster's desk, poor Willy tearfully confessed:

"Twas she herself, sir," sobbed the lad.
"I did not mean to be so bad;
But when Susannah shook her curls
And whispered I was 'fraid of girls
And dussn't kiss a baby's doll,
I couldn't stand it sir, at all,
But up and kissed her on the spot!
I know — boo-hoo — I ought to not;
But, somehow, from her look — boo-hoo —
I thought she kind o'wished me to!"

The verse was of especial interest to the Nobel Prize-winning Robert A. Milliken (1868-1953) because the girl, Susannah Pease, was a relative on his mother's side. And it is told that when, in 1928, Gen. Charles G. Dawes, Calvin Coolidge's vice-president, was introduced to visitors from Stockbridge, he, to their astonishment, recited the opening lines of the poem:

A district school, not far away,
'Mid Berkshire hills, one winter's day,
Was humming with its wonted noise
of three-score mingled girls and boys.

The newsprint "revolution" began in the Berkshires

It has been more than 100 years since the first groundwood pulp made in the United States — indeed, in the Western Hemisphere — was made in Curtisville, a village in Stockbridge now known as Interlaken. But today, beside Route 183 in Interlaken, all that remains of that mill is a burrstone and a plaque to remind us of a momentous event in paper technology.

The importance of groundwood paper resides in its relative cheapness (I keep saying *relative* in connection with cost because all papers, including newsprint, are now sky-high in price), an attribute which makes possible the large-circulation newspapers of today.

Formerly, paper was made from rags, which were in turn made of linen (flax) or cotton. In the mid-19th century, as the country's population increased and urbanization was drawing people into cities, newspapers proliferated, and the supply of rags could not keep pace with the demand. A history of the newspaper in America states: "Newsprint is a prosaic subject, but the ability to make low-cost newsprint from wood pulp, by a process introduced into America from Germany in 1867, was the basic factor in the growth of the daily newspaper."

And so we can see how important was that little wood pulp mill in Curtisville so long ago. It began when a German, Friedrich Gottlieb Keller, observing wasps making their paper-like nests from plant fibers, conceived the idea of grinding up a log of spruce-wood by holding it against a spinning stone wheel (like a grindstone), cooling it with water and grinding it into a slurry. He had Henry Voelter design the machine, and not long after, three men named Pagenstecher — the brothers Rudolph and Albrecht and their cousin Alberto — imported two of them into America. They were accompanied by their operator, Frederick Wurtzbach, who installed them at a vacant mill "privilege" just downstream from the outlet of Stockbridge Bowl, in Curtisville.

There, on March 5, 1867, was made the first groundwood pulp in America. Conveyed to the Smith-Platner mill in Lee, it was made into paper on March 8 in a trial so successful that the paper mill contracted to take all Wurtzbach's output.

The light at the end of the tunnel

In 1826 two canal promoters stood on the top of Hoosac Mountain separating the Northern Berkshire towns of Florida and (North) Adams. They were Alvah Crocker, a paper manufacturer of Fitchburg, and the surveyor Loammi Baldwin; and they were contemplating the barrier it posed to the canal they projected to link Boston with Albany through the northern reaches of Massachusetts.

Said Baldwin: "Mr. Crocker, all I am really doing is to follow the contour of these hills, and God arranged that contour."

Replied Crocker: "Well, if God did that much, why didn't he poke his thumb through this darned mountain and save us all the trouble of trying to make a tunnel?"

It was just half a century later that men, and not God, succeeded in making a tunnel through that flinty mass, and its construction was a triumph of civil engineering.

The Hoosac Tunnel, extending 4.75 miles through Hoosac Mountain between Florida and North Adams, has for a century been regarded as one of the wonders of the county. It has, accordingly, been the subject of a number of booklets and magazine articles over the years. In my own collection is a little pamphlet published just a century ago by Orson Dalrymple of North Adams, containing a map and chart, and which has been a useful source book for subsequent writers.

Begun in 1851, construction was repeatedly delayed by many troubles; machines bought to cut the bore through rock broke down; loose rock, sand and porous mica in the western part of the mountain required a brick lining in the bore; the blasting powder then available was ineffective; the interception of subterranean water courses caused flooding; labor was hard to recruit and retain.

Men were killed by accidents: the worst was when 13 were killed during the drilling of the central shaft of more than a thousand vertical feet so work could proceed in both directions from inside the mountain. The difficulties strengthened opposition in the Legislature; funds were withheld and work suspended for long intervals.

The new Burleigh rock drill proved to be effective, and a large building was erected to house the air compressors; George M. Mowbray demonstrated the superior blasting power of his trinitroglycerine and set up an on-site plant to produce it; a nearby brickyard was established to provide the more than 20 million bricks for the lining in the western part; so exact a method was developed to align the bore that upon completion the center line deviated by but 9/16 of an inch.

My own memory of the Hoosac Tunnel is of a trip through it in the mid-'30s on the Boston and Maine's crack *Minute Man* passenger train, long since a victim of the ubiquitous automobile.

In recent times, it is used somewhat regularly for freight trains, and accommodates an occasional sight-seeing train.

Richmond, Mass.

West Pittsfield, Mass.

Clapp Park, Pittsfield, Mass.

Clapp Park, Pittsfield, Mass.

The Common, Pittsfield, Mass.

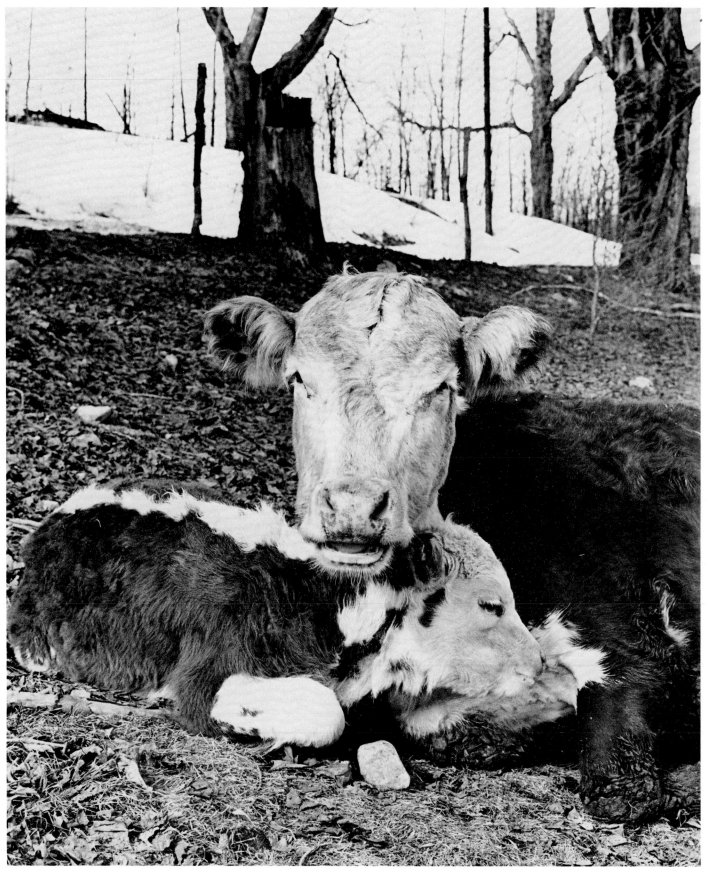

South Mountain Rd., Pittsfield, Mass.

The Common, Pittsfield, Mass.

Pitt Playground, Pittsfield, Mass.

Tanglewood, Lenox, Mass.

Pittsfield, Mass.

Pittsfield, Mass.

Housatonic River, Pittsfield, Mass.

Stockbridge, Mass.

Jacob's Pillow, Becket, Mass.

Tyringham, Mass.

Pittsfield, Mass.

Richmond, Mass.

Lanesboro, Mass.

Pittsfield, Mass.

Lenox, Mass.

Richmond, Mass.

CELEBRATE SUMMER

PHOTOGRAPHS BY
JANE McWHORTER
and
BEVERLY PABST

TEXT BY
RICHARD NUNLEY

Noon

There is a stillness to certain summer noons that gives a hint of what stopped time would be like, or existence without time.

The sun's earliest rays on the mornings of such days lay so palpable a heat on the skin that people outside the post office before 8 a.m. say to each other, "It's going to be a scorcher."

Throughout the forenoon, light and heat intensify, morning song birds disappear and Rover scratches his naphole a little deeper under the lilacs, resting his chin reproachfully on the cool dirt. The lawn grass takes on a limp and rubbery look, and even the stiff and scratchy zinnias begin to wilt. Cud-chewing cows cluster in the shade of pasture oaks or willows, swishing their tails like tassled pashas. It's the sort of morning on which ladies years ago took a sponge bath after household chores were out of the way, and, having prepared a cold dinner and supper, changed into sprigged percale for the rest of the day.

The tractor mowing at the far end of the field half-dissolves in heat shimmer. Flies dance in the shadowy coolness of the open cellarway, and the raspy buzz of the "hot-and-dry bird" (cicadas, actually) grows more insistent as the sun climbs the sky toward noon. The plaintive monotony of cardinals' repeated whistles and the constant commotion of young crows back in the airless pines begins to get on the nerves, and the August world suddenly looks altogether too green and overgrown, and turning on the mental air conditioning, imagination projects white and blue slides of bare February.

Etymologically, noon is the ninth hour after sunrise (from *nona*, Latin for ninth); 3 a.m. seems to me awfully early for sunrise, but perhaps the ancient Roman name-coiners had in mind sunrise in Lapland or Novya Zembla or someplace like that. Canonically, though, the ninth hour was 3 p.m.; midday was the sixth hour. Does this mean that Romans got up earlier than Christians?

Probably what has happened is that the name for the fourth office of the day ("nones") at 3 o'clock was preceded by the midday meal, which by association took the name of "nones," and, as happens when people are hungry, mealtime subtly crept closer and closer to breakfast until, by the 16th century, it had become identified with the middle of the solar day, and thus the name of the meal was transferred to the hour midway between sunrise and sunset. (The seven daily offices, in case you're ever on a quiz program when the question comes up, are matins (or lauds), prime, tierce, sext, nones, vespers and complin.)

By noon, shadows are shrunk to their minimum, and in the unsparing glare colors look harsh and drained. Standing exposed to the noonday sun on such days, I soon feel weak and shaky in the limbs, and a great sleepiness, an incapacity for taking interest, takes over. To Camus, being thus unsheltered from the merciless blaze of noon suggested the position of modern man, who, unable to interpose any comforting parasol of illusion between himself and the searing reality of nothingness, is morally paralyzed and incapable of decision he can believe in.

Noon seems to be the American hour, the hour when the aloneness, the isolation of a human being on an enormous continent and in a thoroughgoingly individualistic society seems epitomized in the characteristic mood of the hour, the mood of a remote barn stuffed with hay-bales drowsing and baking in the sun. It is

alone, apparently forgotten; grasshoppers click; the shadow of its uneven eaves crowds close to its sill, the sense of emptiness, of waiting, the pathos of timelessness and abandon it embodies, almost too poignant to bear.

Willa Cather's fiction is suffused with this American sense of loneliness, this bone-deep on-your-ownness which makes other cultures foreign to us; the contemporary poet William Stafford captures it; so did Theodore Roethke. I fancied I heard it last Wednesday evening in the premier performance by the Berkshire Music Center orchestra under Gunther Schuller of Ramon Zupko's "Sun Dance." Noon is the hour of reverence, of unshadowed confrontation with deepest things, alone and sufficient.

While the sun shines

Summer takes on a certain leonine tawniness about this time. You see it in the metallic luster of the maturing foliage of the trees, but more obviously in the golden toastedness of mown fields and higher pastures where bedrock is not far down. From one hilltop the other day, I saw on a hillside miles off the large, whitish-yellow square of what must be a nearly vertical hayfield hanging like a banner amongst the woods, as if someone were putting out the flag of ripeness.

Now that the first hay is in, farmers can get around to odd-job mowing for people who want their fields kept open but whose blend of witch grass and gold-enrod and yellow flags and milkweed and burdock wouldn't be considered hay even by a goat. Such is our field, but its cuttings make serviceable mulch, especially after wintering over in a great pile.

Haying in my mind seems to stand for introduction to maturity, one of the first jobs a youngster can take part in and feel his or her efforts and labors count for just as much as anyone else's. It is also an introduction to bending to a task and keeping at it until it is done — which is a world away from doing something only for so long as one "feels comfortable with it." Sometimes our modern distaste for seeing ourselves as Simon Legrees deprives our juniors of enlightening experience.

I suppose the experience of forking windrows into haycocks in broiling sun up and down a vast rolling hayfield, and then pitching the haycocks onto the creaking, weather-worn wagon, and then riding atop the slippery, lurching load behind the deliberateness of Dolly and 'Lije in their jingling traces as they plod back to the barn where you suddenly rumble into dark, dusty, tea-scented shadow in which droning flies dance, is a piece of ancient history. You'd have to go to some sort of museum of bygone country life to see it now. But without the necessity, it would be only nostalgic charm, which may be interesting, but is not sustaining. Make-believe leaves you feeling forlorn after a while. Wholehearted effort, the kind that yields durable satisfaction, requires some felt imperative.

After John Deere displaced the grays, tossing hay bales onto a flatbed furnished equal experience of imperatives. Your eyebrows were perpetually heavy with sweat. Your back began to feel like seceded territory under the allied plagues of sunburn, hayseed and greenheads. And your hands (even with gloves) and your off knee began to feel as if an incompetent acupuncturist had been bloodying them as you snatched a bale off the ground waist-high and gave it a hist with the knee up onto the load.

Somewhere along the line of progress,

finger-damaging baling wire gave way to twine; then the baler was adapted to shoot the bales directly into an accompanying wagon, thereby obviating stoop labor. Now even bales are on the way out. Hay is put up in enormous bedrolls now.

And hay itself is less the staple it used to be, as dairy farmers cut green forage (which these days is not just plain old timothy and clover) and either deliver it straightaway to the cows who stay in the ventilated barn or else treat it as silage so that less food value is lost in the preserving. All this makes undeniable sense, both in terms of economics and human drudgery. But one side effect is to elevate the importance of cash (or credit) and demote the importance of humans — and the character of humans.

It's hard, especially for middle-class youngsters, to have an opportunity nowadays to see that it makes a difference whether we work or not — and how we work. Cash, rather than accomplishment, becomes the motive for work. As Marx pointed out years ago, this distances us from the actualities of life. (How, unless work had taken us there, would we ever know the haunting loneliness of the mute shadows of hot pines edging the remote mountain hayfield?) It becomes "cool"

to scoff at conscientious toil.

Every good thing, nevertheless, is the product of work on somebody's part. Popular cant has it that respect for work is a sign of something fishy in the psyche — witness all the sneers about the "puritan work ethic" (even though the originator of the phrase, Max Weber, called it the "*Protestant* work ethic"). Freud observed that work and love are what we need to make us happy souls; we seem conveniently not to have heard the work part. As Robert Frost said, "The world is full of willing people — some willing to work, and others willing to let them."

One of my favorite hymns goes:

Come, labor on.
Who dares stand idle on the harvest plain,
While all around him waves the golden grain.
Away with gloomy doubts and faithless fear!
No arm so weak but may do service here.
Redeem the time; its hours too swiftly fly.
No time for rest, till glows the western sky,
Till the long shadows o'er our pathway lie;
And a glad sound comes with the setting sun:
'Servants, well done.'

Fortunate are those who have work they know they can and must and wish to do.

Jane McWhorter's photographs appear on pages 51-64. Beverly Pabst's photographs appear on pages 68-79.

Monterey, Mass.

51

Monterey, Mass.

New Marlborough, Mass.

Great Barrington Fair

Berkshire County 4-H Fair, Great Barrington, Mass.

Housatonic, Mass.

Great Barrington, Mass.

New Marlborough, Mass.

Berkshire County 4-H Dairy Show, Great Barrington Fair

Sandisfield, Mass.

General Electric Kiddy Day, Pittsfield, Mass.

Southfield, Mass.

Cheshire, Mass.

Lenox, Mass.

Thoreau's night on Greylock

Sometime in July 1844, when he was 27, Thoreau spent a night on top of Mount Greylock, his sole visit, so far as is known, to the Berkshires. He digresses to tell about it in "Tuesday" of *A Week on the Concord and Merrimac* (1849), the book he wrote about a boating excursion he made with his brother in 1839. The night on Greylock was part of the trip he referred to in a letter written back home again in Concord on Aug. 14: "I have but just returned from a pedestrian excursion . . . to the Catskill Mountains, over the principal mountains of this state, subsisting mainly on bread and berries, and slumbering on the mountaintops. As usually happens, I now feel a slight sense of dissipation . . ."

Some dissipation.

He had walked here from Monadnock, following from the Connecticut the Deerfield River, the route of today's Mohawk Trail, up to the height of land, where he spent the night with a Mr. Rice.

Next morning he hiked over Hoosac Mountain and walked down into North Adams, where he stocked up on "a little rice and sugar and a tin cup." (Hawthorne had spent a "get away from it all" vacation in North Adams six years before, from July 26 to Sept. 11, 1838.)

That afternoon Thoreau rambled through farms up the Bellows (presumably the present Reservoir Road out of North Adams), leaving the roundabout path to the summit where it veered right at the next-to-last house.

There he chatted with a woman "unconcernedly combing her long black hair" as she talked. She took him for one of the Williamstown students, "a pretty wild set of fellows," she said.

At the last house, the farmer took him for a peddler, and told him he couldn't get to the top that way, for the slope was "as steep as the roof of a house." Thoreau, confident he knew better, beelined through his cow yard, the farmer shouting after him that he wouldn't get to the top that night.

Susan Denault of Adams, knowledgeable Greylock guide now with the Massachusetts Department of Environmental Management Regional Headquarters on South Mountain, has researched likely cellar holes and old maps and census records. She thinks the woman may have been Rebecca Eddy and the farmer Smith Wilbur.

Thoreau, having fought his way through dense laurel thickets, gained the summit just as the sun was setting, coming out on a clearing of several acres "covered with stumps and rocks," with a sizable wooden observatory in the middle, which Williams students had constructed.

By scraping out a two-foot hole in a damp spot as darkness fell, he got enough water to boil his supper of rice over a fire he made on the observatory floor, "having already whittled a wooden spoon to eat it with." He settled to sleep on a loose board, with other random boards cuddled around him (he had no blanket). He woke very cold in the night, and so put another board on top of himself, held down by a stone. How you balance a board on top of yourself, much less sleep that way, I don't see; clearly, anything is tolerable if you do it of your own accord. Clouds floated through the open upper windows of the observatory through the night.

He got up before dawn to see the sun rise, finding with increasing light an "ocean of mist" lapping the very base of the tower. The entire rest of the world was blanked out, leaving him alone with the sun. Then, following the compass reading he had taken the night before on Pontoosuc, "a fair lake in the southwest," he made his own route down the mountain and walked the rainy 15 miles to Pittsfield. There, by prearrangement, he met his chum William Ellery Channing (the younger) at the depot of the Western Railroad, to continue the excursion by proceeding to Albany, where they took the night river boat down to the Catskills.

Channing later wrote in his copy of *A Week*:"He had no shirt collar perceptible, carried a small leather wallet belonging to the late Charles Emerson on his back, and looked as if he had slept out in the fields as he was unshaved & drest very poorly."

One glittering and breezy morning last week we drove up the Notch Road to commemorate his visit. The mowing crew at the summit was bundled up in windbreakers, though the sun was bright. Clearly visible in the northeast were blue Wachusett (67 miles away) and Monadnock (57 miles) where Thoreau had walked from, and in the southwest the bold pile of the Catskills (57 miles), where he was going. The towns and cities of Berkshire were just a little pale bloom dusted on the green levels tucked between the immensely rumpled broadloom of the broken terrain.

In Bascom Lodge we ate an enormous and delicious cranberry muffin and a cup of coffee — no plain boiled rice for us. By firelight Thoreau had read with interest the ads in the scraps of newspaper left there; last week the kitchen crew was enjoying the excellent reception of TV ads and soap operas on the summit. A young gray cat yawned in the white-curtained window as we left.

We didn't feel dissipated at all; on the contrary, there was a spiritual elation to being there. Having a mountain in our midst ennobles life the way meeting someone genuinely good elevates the day — if we will remember to go up it now and then.

In his journal on June 28, 1852, Thoreau wrote, "I have camped out all night on the tops of four mountains — Wachusett, Saddleback [meaning Greylock], Ktaadn and Monadnock — and I usually took a ramble over the summit by moonlight. I remember the moaning of the wind on the rocks, and that you seemed much nearer to the moon than on the plains. The light is then in harmony with the scenery . . . From the cliffs you looked off into vast depths of illumined air."

Arlo Guthrie, singer, at Alice Brock's wedding, Housatonic, Mass.

Alice May Brock, author, restaurateur, Housatonic, Mass.

Louis Kahn, architect, Stockbridge, Mass.

Erik Erikson, psychiatrist, Stockbridge, Mass.

Arthur Penn, film and stage director, Housatonic, Mass.

William Gibson, playwright, Stockbridge, Mass.

Eugene Ionesco, playwright, Stockbridge, Mass.

Norman Mailer, author, Stockbridge, Mass.

Yousuf Karsh, photographer, at the home of Norman Mailer, Stockbridge, Mass.

Leonard Bernstein, Tanglewood, Lenox, Mass.

Up on the berrying ground

In the Berkshires, as in New England generally, there are certain things one just doesn't come right out with in front of everybody. Things such as where unfailing trout pools are, or choice blueberry grounds.

I could feel something within me gasp with shock the other night at the Greylock campfire when naturalist Mike Van Dyke announced in unhushed, public tones that blueberry picking at Jones's Nose was the best around. (Incidentally, can you imagine coming home with a pailful and saying, "I've been picking Jones's Nose"?) Such bald publication of what should be private confidences takes some getting used to; there's no call to tell *everything* you know on a first meeting.

I go into this by way of pointing up, for those unacquainted hereabouts, how grave a matter blueberrying is. Blueberrying is not merely an occasion for a pleasant excursion; there's something ancestral about it. You wouldn't feel comfortable if blueberry season had come and gone and you hadn't lifted finger or foot toward getting as many as you could. I don't call this greed; I call it gratitude. The berries are there, clustered plump and blue under their light green, melonseed-shaped leaves amongst the hardhack and sweet fern; and what could be more the mark of an ingrate than to let such delectable abundance go by and dry up and not be appreciated? I'd be rather put out if I were God and people paid no more attention to my productions than that.

Illogically perhaps, this sense of sacred obligation doesn't apply to cultivated blueberries, nor to raspberries or elderberries, currants or even strawberries — only to wild blueberries. (A true Berkshirite's attitude toward strawberries is an entirely different variety of religious experience; not negligible, but different. Berlioz and Bach are both inestimable composers, but your inner feel for Berlioz you would never for a second confuse with your inner feel for Bach. That's how it is with blueberries and strawberries.)

Why this particular feeling attaches to wild blueberries and nothing else, it would be interesting to know. Some cannier theorist of rituals than I ought to tackle the problem. Maybe he would say it's a holdover from way back when you had to gather blueberries to survive the winter, but I think a drippy theory like that would give anthropology a bad name. Maybe he would say it's because berrying is a family undertaking, and we invest it with the holiness that attaches to the security of our identity, which comes out of family. That doesn't sound like anybody I know, either. Maybe it is greed, after all.

I know (and my groaning family knows even better) that once I get onto "our" blueberry ground (I'll go so far as to reveal it's within 50 miles of Park Square), it's hard for me to leave. There are always a few more too good to pass up. As pint becomes quart, and quart slowly but surely swells to gallon, I calculate and recalculate the number of blueberry pies, muffins, pancakes, and grunts we can count on. No Wall Street *conglomerateur* ever counted his unhatched chickens so carefully. Yet however many we pick, we never come down with enough.

And what if somebody else should come and clean out the patch before we have a chance to return for more? I feel the mountain tremble under my feet at that alarming thought, the sun-blushed cheek turn pale.

Robert Frost has a nice poem on the subject, aptly entitled "Blueberries," in which the speaker tells how naively, when a newcomer to town, he asked Loren, a native whose family practically supported themselves on picking berries, if he knew of a good place to go berrying. "He said he'd be glad to tell if he knew . . . He spoke to his wife in the door, 'Let me see, Mame, we don't know any good berrying place?' It was all he could do to keep a straight face."

Emerson when a student at Harvard tiptoed away to go berry picking at Mount Auburn. (A lot happened at Mount Auburn, for a cemetery; Pierce Butler romanced Fanny Kemble there.) And Thoreau was famous for leading blueberry expeditions. It was the first thing he did after being let out of jail for not paying his poll tax. Winslow Homer did a marvelous watercolor in 1873 of berry pickers with their lard pails picking in the lee of granite boulders on a breezy day by the ocean, with a companionable blackbird whistling from a bleached dead branch.

Maybe the specialness of wild blueberries is that they grow in marginal places, on moors by the ocean or on top of hills, and you have to go to extremes to get them. Our wildnesses are not for everybody to know about.

CELEBRATE AUTUMN

PORTRAITS OF A BERKSHIRE VILLAGE

PHOTOGRAPHS BY
NIKI BERG

TEXT BY
KATHARINE H. ANNIN

Down on the Farm

Looking back 40 years and more to days when Sabine Farm was in the milk-producing business, I can't help thinking how shocked my husband would be to see so many fields all around the county that are still standing full of dry brown cornstalks, their growing season brought to an end several weeks ago by the first hard frost. He would be astonished that so many farmers had been taken unprepared by a sudden drop in temperature, and horrified to see them thus lose such a large part of the winter's food they had counted on for their herds of cattle.

Nothing shows more vividly, for all to see, that farming has undergone tremendous changes in the last few decades. In the old days, the chief operation of autumn was "filling silo," and the trick was to let your corn go on maturing as long as possible but still cut it before, or immediately after, the first killing frost. From Labor Day on, preparations were made among cooperative neighbors to share their machinery and their teams of horses with each other at a moment's notice. After Sept. 15, we considered ourselves lucky if the frost held off.

Some silos were built of metal by the time we joined the back-to-the-land movement, but ours was of narrow, vertical tongue-and-groove strips of wood, and was once blown down by a late summer twister, the nearest thing to a tornado we ever had in this vicinity, until the real one that hit West Stockbridge in 1973. At silo-filling time, the curved top of a tall pipe was fitted into an opening in the roof, and through this pipe the chopped ensilage was blown by the tractor-driven chopping machine. This was constantly fed by a steady parade of wagons that brought the loads of cornstalks in from the fields, the corn-harvesting machine having cut and tied them into bundles with baling twine.

All these machines made it into a noisy operation, but I remember the anxiety with which I used to listen from the house for a sudden silence which might indicate that some part of the machinery had broken down. If so, a trip to Albany might be required to find a spare part, which would mean a disastrous delay. But once in the silo, the corn turned into a nourishing supplement to their hay and grain that cows seemed to find palatable, though it was hard to see why.

With the steady decline in dairy farming in the Berkshires after World War II, it was left to the big farms in the Midwest to make the improvements in farm methods that revolutionized milk production. While our hillside pastures and rocky fields were left to grow up to new forest, out there the huge farms of level acreage were ideal for the big, expensive combines that did the work of many farm-hands, in half the time.

Breeding practices have come a long way, too, in developing big producers among cows. By studying lines of ancestry, and adopting the most scientific feeding programs, dairy farmers have made great progress. The average cow in 1980 is said to have produced 12,000 pounds of milk a year, whereas in 1960 the average production was 8,000, quite an increase in 20 years.

The cow, however, may not have lived such a pleasant life as she would have had she been born 20 years earlier. For instead of roaming green pastures and drinking from bubbling streams, at least in summer, she is likely to have lived exclusively in a barn, where she can get a controlled, balanced diet that will get the maximum of protein into her. At milking time, she will be ushered into the "milking parlor" where she will stand next to her milking attendant who will be in a waist-deep pit arranged for his convenience in attaching the vacuum cups of the milking machine to the cow's udder.

Rob Rathbun, retired farmer: *"Yup, this is my room. I live like the cows now. Eat and sleep in the same place."*

Julia Rodda, housewife: *"I start in the morning at 5:30 with cleaning out the barn. Yes, there's no end to the chores around here."*

Henry Rodda, retired farmer: *"Ma Rodda takes care of about everything around here now."*

An old-time skill I should like to see revived is using a scythe correctly. I saw a picture in the press last summer that made me cringe. It showed a man supposedly cutting tall grass, but his scythe, evidently at the end of a sweeping stroke, was level with his shoulders, where a scythe should never be. The trick is to keep the blade flat to the ground as you pull it, by a quick jerk of both wrists, toward you, through the grass or whatever you intend to cut. An essential part of scything, also, is knowing how to use a whetstone, an art in itself, and more exercise for wrists. A farmer once told me that when his men used to scythe large fields of grain they sharpened their tools on the grindstone twice a day and touched them up about every 20 minutes with the whetstones they carried in their pockets. In fact, a whet originally meant "a spell of work between two whettings of a scythe."

For years, too, I have been regretting the passing of those pleasant institutions with which the Berkshires used to be dotted before they were superseded by the cocktail lounge.

It was so restful to stop in for a cup of tea in the late afternoon on the way home from more strenuous activities, or to take a friend with you for a quiet chat, uninterrupted by the telephone or the goings and comings of the rest of the household. The tearooms I remember best were run by ladies in their own homes: like Mrs. Breen's in Stockbridge, and the Misses Malcolm's Orchard Tea Garden in West Pittsfield, and the wide veranda of a summer home, near ours, where two college girls served passersby for several summers.

Part of the relaxed atmosphere stemmed from the fact that customers were not required to make up their minds between dozens of beverages. You were offered *tea*; your choice lay only between sugar, lemon and real cream. It was usually accompanied by dainty sandwiches and a sweeter confection all made by the hostess herself; though I recall that Mrs. Breen specialized in small hot rolls, just out of the oven and dripping with butter. No one thought about calories in those days.

Nellie Cameron, retired schoolteacher: *"I taught the last graduating class of the Shaker children, so you know how long I've been around."*

Karl Hanson, restaurant owner

Gunnar Hanson, retired carpenter

Ruth Whitman, wife of former town clerk: *"My father was the minister here. He lived in the parsonage. I got married there too."*

Perry Whitman, retired town clerk: *"I was town clerk for forty-two years, and I'm darn proud of it."*

In spite of all that is wrong with the world, human nature must be fundamentally optimistic. That is if we judge by the number of cheerful sayings in our language about clouds having silver linings and blessings in disguise and admonitions to turn evil into good, as though that were entirely possible. So it is with our deep Berkshire winters.

A few days of temperatures above 32 degrees last week were enough to arouse hope that winter was relaxing its hold, and a few maple-syrup enthusiasts went as far as to hang out their buckets. It seemed reasonable to expect the weather to cooperate by supplying a few sunny, mild days, alternating with cold nights, such as are needed for a "good run of sap."

Around here, Washington's birthday (the real one on Feb. 22) used to be considered the most likely date for driving in the spouts, with care to hang only as many pails on one maple tree as the diameter of its trunk warrants, never more than four, and on the side of the trunk that gets the most sun.

With spouts and pails installed, you are at the mercy of the weather. By the way, if you want to be considered a connoisseur, you must refer to the spouts as spiles, just as you must call the old-time kitchen-living room the keeping room, and the wooden shingles on the roof, shakes.

However, I notice Alice Morse Earle, the 19th-century authority on Colonial times, calls them spouts. She describes sugar making before pails were available, when a gash was chopped along the side of the tree and scooped out to collect the sap.

But this method sometimes killed the tree, and had to be abandoned.

So, by trial and error, small holes came to be fitted with basswood spouts, made by a special tool called a tapping-gauge, to guide the dripping sap into troughs dug out of logs, Indian fashion. This was still a long way from the modern method of attaching plastic pipe lines at the tree trunk, which deliver the liquid directly to the boiling vats and evaporators.

Thus has been eliminated, little by little, the laborious intermediate task of transporting it over snow-covered ground, originally by yokes over men's shoulders, then on sleds pulled by oxen or horses and later by tractors if the ground was smooth enough.

Over the years, also, the final stages in the long process of boiling sap into syrup, and syrup into sugar, have been refined by the use of every sort of mechanical and electrical improvement; and the uniform testing and grading and marketing of the end product have come under government control, with the inevitable rise in price to astronomical heights. In spite of labor-saving methods, only a quarter as much making of maple syrup goes on today as in early days.

But still the popularity of maple products as luxury items has kept alive this old-time rural occupation. I hear that in New Hampshire maple trees are being rented during the sap season, for 15 cents a tap, in the state forests and by private owners of maple groves, to people anxious to utilize them. Who knows where the law of supply and demand may lead?

Howard Whitman, retired farmer: *"This is a great stove. They made the legs that size so there'd be enough room for a wet dog or your wet boots."*

ALICE F. JONES
1904 — 1964

Emerald Jones, caretaker: *"Here's my wife's grave, and my son's. He died in Korea. I lost them a long time ago."*

Rob Rathbun

Mrs. J. Alhert, widow: *"My religion and my memories keep me happy now."*

Charles Christensen

The Berkshire landscape has changed markedly in the last few decades, which is to say, since farming has declined. Hayfields and pastures are on their way to reverting to woodlands, and especially missed are the cows that used to keep hedgerows and fence lines neatly cropped. Many vistas of near or distant hills once visible as one drove about are obliterated by roadside growth.

For that very reason, perhaps, I am more conscious of the immediate edges of our highways and of the backroads I like to patronize whenever they lead to my destination without adding perceptible mileage and gas consumption; which is quite often if I check with my odometer or a map. As I am not given to high speeds on any roads, I consequently can enjoy whatever wildflowers the highway department has left. And there are a good many, in spite of its efforts to "clean up" the roadsides. At least the use of weed-killing sprays that turned all vegetation brown has been abandoned.

I can't proceed at the slow speed of old Dobbin in the days of horse and buggy, and I often think of the late Rev. Henry Sherrill, who spent the summers of his boyhood here in Richmond, and used to tell how, when he took his mother for a drive, she would say, "Stop the horse and let me out. I think I see a four-leaf clover." At least I can spot the tall and bright-colored species from the car. At this stage in summer's progress, goldenrod and asters are coming into bloom, and joe-pye weed is conspicuous in lower, damp ground.

Bessie Roberts, housewife: *"I hurt my knee in the spring but don't worry about me. I'm a tough old bird."*

Reuben Johnson, dairy farmer: *"My cows are like my babies. They need caring for and looking after all the time."*

Dudley Williams, hired farmhand: *"I ain't havin' no picture taken . . . why do you want a picture of me anyway?"*

Oliver W. Osborne kept his diary meticulously, without skipping a day, and when I had perused his records for the winter of 1876-1877, I felt that I was well acquainted with him. He used long, ruled pages, big enough to accommodate a month on a page, with a line for each day and several left at the bottom for a succinct comment on the month as a whole. His writing was small but legible, with especially noteworthy items standing out in larger, blacker and fancier penmanship.

Mr. Osborne managed to record an amazing amount of activity by writing in terse phrases rather than complete sentences; his is not at all the discursive sort of diary we associate with his contemporaries in the 19th century. It is more literally a Line-a-Day book than those journals that adopted that title years later. His spelling, while not always consistent, was more correct than his overuse of capitals and his almost complete lack of punctuation.

Like all good farmers, Mr. Osborne was very conscious of the weather. Every day's entry begins with a weather report, such as Clear, Frosty, Mild and Still, Began to snow, Squirts of Rain, Eve clear But wind hauled South. There often follow comments on road conditions: New Snow soft but the old is hard and will bear a Horse [in February]; Road bad snow banks and Mud [in April]. He evidently lived far enough from Lenox to hitch up his horse every time he went there, which was often. In fact, he makes so many references to going to the post office that I thought he might have had a job there, until he referred to going "to P O after books." He was forever taking books to different people, sometimes as far away as Pittsfield, or going to get books from them. He must have been a book agent for some publisher, but what kind of books they were remains a mystery.

It is equally hard to figure out who resided with him. I assume a lady referred to as E was his wife. He frequently carried E to see this or that neighbor, or to attend the funerals of several oldsters whose deaths he recorded, at ages in the 70s and 80s. ("Carrying," as you may know, was a common synonym in old documents for "driving"; indeed he carried so many people hither and yon, that perhaps he conducted a sort of livery stable on the side.)

Another person besides E appears so often in these annals, and took part in so many of our hero's farming activities that I took him to be a son, or brother or a hired man. He is referred to merely as Cha's. But when I read that Cha's Well failed, and that Cha's began to shingle his barn, I decided he was a near neighbor with whom Osborne was on intimate terms. The two of them cooperated in day-to-day activities of what we would call subsistence farming. Distant events concerned him not at all, or not enough to deserve comment, except for the entry on Mar. 5, 1877; Hayes Inaugurated. On Apr. 2, he did attend Town Meeting, but says nothing more about it.

Almost every day, Osborne mentions that he sawed wood. One winter day, he cut an ash tree, and Hauled wood from barn to wood H. [House?]. He had the usual country water problems: Jan. 28 Water gone in barn cistern again, but on Mar. 9 Cistern full water in Well Dry since Oct. 18. From early spring, his entries are full of preparing his north garden and his south garden, of planting every sort of vegetable, and watching them sprout and grow, of finding 22 potato Bugs June 1, and 38 the next day. He cut asparagus May 10, and set a hen on 17 eggs. Moreover, he took time to record, in his special large lettering, the arrival of every spring bird, and on April 8 the appearance of Frogs in Mr. Judd's pond. [Could they have been spring peepers?]

But now hear this; May 24, 1877, Mr. Osborne writes, "Snowing at daylight snow hard till 8 a m 3 inches. Bartletts hills white at noon Bald Head white all day. I rolled 2 balls of Snow size of Large Barrells under apple tree in full Blossom Thursday morning it lasted till Saturday Aft. Good sledding on grass ground, Corn looking up out of Snow."

It wasn't till May 30 that he Turned Cow out.

George Whitman, retired farmer: *"I know the little red potatoes cost more money in the store, but you can take the biggest ones. Where I come from it's the bigger the better."*

It used to be said that the way to insure yourself of a long life was to choose long-lived parents. So perhaps it is natural that I have never given much thought to old age, since I come from a long-lived tribe. I am not yet as old as my father lived to be, and he had an aunt who topped 98. When I was a child, there were always white-haired relatives coming and going, and while they may not all have been as old as I took them to be, they were surely what was called "well along in years."

For myself, I have never thought much about the passing of the years.

ABOUT THE PHOTOGRAPHERS

NIKI BERG, of New York City and Hancock, Massachusetts, studied for three years at the International Center for Photography. In 1977 she won third prize in a *Redbook* sponsored photography competition. More recently she was a first prize winner in Either/Or Press's first annual "Life in the Berkshires" photography contest. Her work has been seen around the Berkshires at the Honey Sharp Gallery, the Berkshire Museum (December '82), Simon's Rock College, and in Hancock Village where a group of her distinctive portraits are on permanent display in the Town Hall. Her work has also been exhibited at Soho Photo, N.Y.U. Photo Center Gallery, Women-books Gallery, and the 14th Street YMHA — all in New York City. A bold new series of color prints featuring nude studies of mothers and daughters has been exhibited at the Simon Gallery in Montclair, New Jersey. The drive to capture the "essential" person she photographs characterizes the body of her work. She lives with her husband Peter and two daughters, Jessica and Karina.

JOEL LIBRIZZI was born and raised in Pittsfield, Massachusetts, and, but for a year at Ohio State University and four years in Europe with the U.S. Army, he has been in the Berkshires ever since. In 1960 he became a news and feature photographer for *The Berkshire Eagle*, where he is still employed. His pictures, however, have been seen the world over in publications including *Esquire, U.S. News & World Report, Woman's Day, Newsweek, Yankee*, and the *New York Times Magazine*. His book credits include Stefan Lorant's *Pittsburgh*, and the works of physical-culturist Bonnie Prudden. He is also the recipient of numerous news photography awards. Joel Librizzi has three children: Marcus, Tara, and David.

JANE McWHORTER has been a professional photographer and graphic artist since 1962. She "escaped to the Berkshires" from her native Brooklyn in 1969. In 1976 she joined with filmmaker John MacGruer to form Blue Sky Productions, a full service visual communications studio in Sandisfield, Massachusetts. She exhibits her work regularly at galleries and museums throughout the Berkshires, and her most recent series of hand-painted black and white photographs has received critical and popular acclaim. She has taught photography at Berkshire Community College, at the DeSisto School in Stockbridge, Massachusetts, and at The School of Visual Arts in New York City. Her book designing credits include Alice May Brock's *My Life As A Restaurant*, and Jill Freedman's *Resurrection City*.

BEVERLY PABST, who now makes her home in Stockbridge, Massachusetts, studied photography with Professor Arthur Freed at Pratt Institute. Her pictures have been seen in New York City and Berkshire galleries, and have been published in *Saturday Review, The New York Times, Playboy, Boston Magazine*, and others. Her book credits include *The Two Faces Of Ionesco* by Rosette C. Lamont and M.J. Friedman, *The Berkshire Anthology, I and II*, and an as yet unpublished work entitled *White Shadows* with a text by Eugene Ionesco. She is currently working on two other books of photographs, one of which will be written by Ms. Pabst. She finds in black and white photography allusions to metaphysical questions beyond the particular image. So long as photography continues "to invite her to this dimension of sight as insight," she will "follow this thin thread of light as is now lent me."

ABOUT THE WRITERS

KATHARINE ANNIN was as inevitable a choice to be a contributor to this book as she was to write the award-winning history of *Richmond, Massachusetts: the Story of a Berkshire Town and Its People*. For some eight decades she has taken part in the life of Richmond and of the larger Berkshire community — as summer resident, farm-dweller, teacher, librarian and writer, in addition to being wife, mother, and grandmother. With her husband, William Stuart Annin, she moved in 1924 to one of Richmond's oldest farms, where William raised Guernsey cattle and Katharine Annin still lives. After her husband's death in 1957, she continued a Tuesday column for *The Berkshire Eagle*, which Mr. Annin had written for sixteen years.

RICHARD NUNLEY was born in Cohasset, Massachusetts in 1931. He attended Dartmouth College, from which he was graduated in 1953, and then studied at Cambridge University, graduating in 1955. In 1957 he came to the Berkshires and took up teaching at the Darrow School in New Lebanon, New York, where he remained until 1970. He has been teaching at Berkshire Community College in Pittsfield ever since. He has been writing for the "Our Berkshires" column since 1980. He lives in New Lebanon with his two daughters and his wife Susan, who is a photographer and piano instructor at the Pittsfield Community Music School.

GERARD CHAPMAN was born in Chicago on the eve of World War I. He was graduated from the Massachusetts Institute of Technology in 1937, and spent much of his career in research laboratories, most recently at the Schweitzer Division of Kimberly-Clark Corporation in Lee, Massachusetts. In the Berkshires, he has lived in the towns of Great Barrington, Mill River, Lee, and Stockbridge, where he now resides. In 1962 his history of Great Barrington's St. James' Church was published by the parish. He has contributed pieces to *The Berkshire Eagle, The Berkshire Courier, The Berkshire Sampler,* and *Berkshires Week*. Since 1977 he has contributed pieces to *The Eagle's* "Our Berkshires" column, focusing chiefly on historical subjects. He has written also "William Cullen Bryant — The Cummington Years," published in 1980. He has one son and three daughters, two of whom remain in the Berkshires. Mr. Chapman lives with his second wife, Edith W. Lloyd of Stockbridge, Massachusetts.

ORDERING PRINTS

Prints of the photographs contained in this book are available through Either/Or Press or from the photographers directly.

Joel Librizzi, Berkshire Eagle, 33 Eagle Street, Pittsfield, Mass. 01201;

Niki Berg, 143 West 95th Street, New York, NY 10025;

Jane McWhorter, Blue Sky Productions, Sandisfield, Mass. 01255;

Beverly Pabst, P.O. Box 123, Stockbridge, Mass. 01262

Either/Or Press

Either/Or Press was born in the Berkshires in 1982. It is meant as a vehicle in which the creative output of the area's writers and photographers and artists will be delivered to the community at large.

Either/Or Press will consider your ideas for publication projects if you will contribute articulate proposals. Send them to:

Editorial Department
Either/Or Press
122 North Street
Pittsfield, MA 01201